MDLG Bedtime Stories 2

A collection of erotic lesbian age play short stories for ABDL and the Mommy Dommes who love them

By Tina Moore

Table of Content

Mommy To The Rescue

I had loved the woods ever since I could remember. The smell of the pine trees, the soft cool dirt between my toes, and the clean air always made me feel so free. Growing up in the city, I had sworn I would move out into the woods the first chance I could, and it wasn't more than six months ago that the chance finally presented itself. A small wood cabin surrounded by thick bush became available, and I had just the right amount of savings to put down the deposit. I packed up all my things, resigned from my job as a stripper, and moved into the small country community. I got a new job at the local Baker, and although the pay was a significant cut, I was happy to finally be living a simple country life. The only thing I needed now was a dog. I had decided to buy a big mountain dog, the kind that would keep the wolves away and had contacted a breeder about two hours away. She had a new litter of Russian Bear dogs, and I just knew I had to have one.

"Oh, she is so sweet, I'll take her," I said to the owner as I picked up the largest chocolate brown female. She had caramel markings around her eyes and on her chest and tail, and I was in love. She snuggled into me, and after paying the woman and filling out the required paperwork, I took my new little pup home.

"I think I'm going to call you Katya," I said to her as I put her in her travel crate. I climbed into my big black truck and knew that Katya would be riding in the back tray in no time.

"Gosh, you are a big girl," I said to her once we reached the cabin and taking her out I let her sniff the air. She barked happily, and I watched as she sniffed the boundary of the fence.

"Clever girl, come on," I said, opening the door as the first of the winter snow began to fall.

Life progressed calmly and predictably with Katya going to puppy school and graduating the first in her class. I continued to work at the bakery and had made a few friends with the locals. Everything was going along simply until one afternoon when I took Katya out for a walk. We had gone about 3 miles into the forest when Katya alerted me that something was not right. At first, I thought it was a wolf and took my rifle down from my back and held it ready. I let Katya off her leash, but she stayed beside me. I could feel my heart beating hard under my thick winter jacket and stepped slowly, making my boots stomp. Katya sniffed the air, and before I could tell her to stop, she was racing forward into the woods. I began to run after her but stopped when I saw what she had found. She had run about half a mile, and by the time I caught up to her, my legs were tired from running through the snow. I panted as I watch Katya sniff the tree and quickly slung my rifle back onto my back. I reached out and touched the half-naked girl Katya had found. She had been tied to a tree with a rope that was done up too tight for her as her breaths came out in short but labored moans. Her body was exposed to the harsh snow and wind and looking at her near blue legs; I could tell she had been there for a while.

"Sweetheart, who did this to you," I asked as I took my knife from my belt and cut the ropes off her wrists. I held her up as her legs gave way underneath her and commanded Katya to make sure there was no one else out there. I took my jacket off and wrapped it in her smaller frame as I carried her back to my cabin, followed shortly after by Katya. The girl was older than 18 by the number of tattoos on her body, and she turned in my arms as I carried her back to the cabin and snuggled into my generous breast.

"Warm," she softly said, her voice hoarse from the cold. We got back to the cabin, and I was happy I had left the fire burning. Katya went to lay next to it immediately, and I placed the girl down on the sofa in front of it while I added logs to it until the flames were high. I made a hot pot of tea and put my things away before bringing the girl a mug of tea. I placed mine down on the coffee table and held the mug to her mouth, helping her to drink. She coughed, and I hoped that the liquid wouldn't hurt her frozen throat. Katya began to sleep, snoring by the fire as I took the girl in my arms and held her against my body, trying to warm her. However, innocent my intentions where I was still enjoying having such a beautiful helpless girl in my arms, and I pulled my heavy jacket around her firmly.

"My name is Kalista, what's yours?" I asked the girl stroking her hair. She looked up at me and cleared her throat a few times before she spoke.

"I'm Summer," she replied with an angelic voice. Her lips had begun to turn a rosy pink as her body warmed up, and her eyes were focused.

"How did I get here? Who are you?" Summer asked as if suddenly realizing she was not tied to a tree anymore.

"My dog Katya found you. You were tied to a tree, only wearing your um panties and bra. What happened to you?" I replied. Hearing her name, Katya woke up and came to rest her big head next to Summer's thigh, monstering it in contrast. Summer reached out and patted Katya, who craned her neck to meet her touch.

"I was living in the commune; I don't think it is from around here. Where I was, it wasn't snowing. But I tried to escape. The last thing I remember was that I was running through the woods and felt a pinch," Summer said, feeling her arm. She turned it around to try and see the back of it, and sure enough, there was a needle prick in her flesh.

"Those bastards," Summer said as she began to cry. Seeing her upset, Katya began to lick her hand, and I grabbed her by the opening of the jacket and pulled her onto my lap.

"It's OK Summer; you're safe now, we can go to the police and get this all sorted out if you'd like?" I said to her as her little body shook in my arms. I snapped my fingers, and Katya went to lay back down by the fire as I stood up and held Summer in my arms.

"Come on, baby girl, it's alright," I said as I gently rocked her. She reached up, wrapped her arms around my neck, and I felt my blue and white flannel soak through as she cried into the nape of my neck. I walked over to where my phone was laying on the kitchen table and dialed 911 and was told to come down to the station right away. Summer didn't want to go, but I told her that if anything had happened to her while she was unconscious, the police needed to know. I held her hand while they did the relevant tests and asked her if there was anybody they could ring for her. She shook her head, "I'm an orphan, and I never really had any friends. I went to live with the family when I was 18."

"How old are you now?" I asked Summer who had been given baggy clothes from the police. She pushed up the sleeves of the oversized sweater and thought for a moment.

"We didn't celebrate birthdays, but I kept a page with all my important dates, and I know I'm 22," Summer said, trying to remember what she had written in her diary. I told the police she could stay with me to which Summer eagerly agreed, and the

Police said her they would be in touch if they needed anything else or if they could catch the people who had done this to her.

As we walked back to the truck, Katya stood up in the tray and barked happily to us. Summer reached up and cuddled her before I took her hand and pushed her into the truck. Her clothes were four sizes too big, and I looked over at her trying to fold up the jeans around her ankles as I drove out of the station.

"We are going to need to get you some new clothes, little one," I said to her making her giggle. It was the first time I had heard her laugh, and it warmed my heart. But she made my heart skip a beat when she placed her hand over mine.

"Thanks, Kalista. You're so nice to me, and you don't even know me," Summer almost whispered. I gave her a sideward smirk and winked at her, making her giggle again, and I turned my hand over and held hers while I drove us to the store.

"Get whatever you like, you'll need at least five outfits, sweetie," I said, taking a shopping trolley and walking her into the store. Summer went quiet and shy and walked behind me, almost hugging my back. I turned around and looked down at her, only just realizing that she probably hadn't been in a real store in years.

"It's OK baby, do you think I'm going to let anything bad happen to you?" I asked her. She just bit her bottom lip and shook her head before I opened my arms and held her until she gently pushed me away and began to look through the store. I stayed by her as she put in jeans, sweaters, and long sleeve shirts. I took her to the shoe department and got her a pair of winter boots for walking in the woods and a pair for going into town. She chose pink cloud pajamas, and I bought her three pairs of fluffy thigh-high socks and a selection of bras and panties. I liked dressing her, she would twirl in the dressing rooms and playfully pose, and I had to remind myself that she wasn't my baby girl.

I have had baby girls before, but I hadn't bothered looking for one around here, I had figured that my small little country community was too conservative to be into something like this. But here Summer was, giggling when I pulled on her jeans up and playfully spanked her bottom.

"I've been a good girl, why am I getting spanked?!" Summer giggled. I grabbed her wrist and moved her arms out of my way as I struck her one last time.

"Because I like hearing your giggles little one," I whispered in her ear, making her blush. I didn't want her to let me have her just because I had looked after her since Katya found her, so I stepped back and let her dress.

"If you want to leave, just let me know. OK, I'm not about to try and lock you up like they did Summer," I said seriously. Summer turned around and caught me off guard as she wrapped her arms around me and placed her head on my large breasts.

"I know, but you are so nice, you're like a Mommy. I don't

want to leave you," she replied, making me have to clench my calves so I wouldn't push her down and have my way with her right there on the changing room floor. I thought for a minute and swallowed hard before I spoke again.

"I can be your Mommy if you'd like, baby girl," I said softly, hoping that no one else heard. Summer stopped being playful and looked at me very seriously. She took in my larger frame, and full curves, she reached up and ran her hands through my long wavy hair and over my lips.

"OK, Mommy," she quietly whispered, letting her hands rest on my heavy tits. I had thought it was a good idea to get them done while I was stripping but had felt self-conscious of their huge size before now. Now I had a baby girl who didn't know it yet but would be loving them for hours to come. I smiled and paid for Summer's new clothes before she went back into the changing room to dress. When she came out, I was impressed with my baby. She had happily accepted everything that I had told her I wanted her to have, and she looked divine.

"My perfect baby," I said as I took her hand and looked at her. She wore pink snow boots with skinny black denim jeans, a white, long sleeve shirt under a fluffy white sweater. She had a black puffer vest, and I took her hands and pulled on pink fingerless gloves.

"Come here, my little snow bunny," I said, cuddling her and running my hands over her body, making her giggle and squirm in my arms.

"Summer, I'm home, baby girl," I called as I walked into the cabin. It had been two months since I had rescued Summer from the snow and took her in as my little one. We had a good routine of me going to work five days a week, and I had begun to diaper Summer in the evenings. I had told her she was ready to get a job so she didn't get bored during the day and she had been employed at the clothing store we had gone to when I bought her first sets of clothes.

"I'm in here, Mommy," Summer said. I hung my bag up on one of the hooks by the door and thought it was strange that Katya wasn't already by my heel. She usually pounced on us when we came home, and I looked in front of the fireplace, assuming she was there instead. I narrowed my eyes and smiled when I heard Summer's giggles coming from her playroom. I had let one of the rooms of the cabin be for her, and although we slept in my bed together, she spent a lot of time in her playroom.

"Look, Mommy, Katy and I are playing hairdressers," Summer said proudly. I looked at what she had done to Katya and laughed. Katy was not as amused, but I was impressed she had let Summer play for as long as they had. Summer had given Katy two big pink bows on both her ears and had put little butterfly clips over her back. Upon seeing me, Katy looked in my direction with big sad puppy dog eyes and huffed before licking

Summer and putting her head down on the ground as Summer placed more clips in place.

"I think she might have had little enough one, come here and let Mommy get you ready for beddys," I said, clapping my hands at Summer and picking her up. She leaned back as I carried her to the bathroom and tried to put clips in my hair.

"Not on Mommy baby girl, Mommy doesn't want to play right now," I told Summer. Summer looked at me, confused.

"Why not, Mommy?" She asked, stopping like a good girl when I told her no. I sat on the edge of the big bathtub and placed her on my lap before I started running the warm bathwater. I lifted Summer's arms as I took off her shirt, and I flicked her nipples until she was forced to pull away from me.

"Because baby girl, Mommy wants to play with you instead," I said, rubbing her over her soft cotton shorts. It had been her day off today, and she had let the fire burn all day, resulting in a very warm house. I liked it when she did this because she would only wear thigh high socks, short little shorts, and a long sleeve tight shirt making me want to ruin her.

I took off her clothes and stuck two fingers into her mouth, making her choke while she tried to get them as wet as she could. She had made the mistake of not getting my fingers wet enough before and had not repeated the same mistake since. Taking my fingers out of her mouth, I toyed with her asshole making her eyes go wide.

"I think I'm going to fill this pretty little hole tonight baby girl, maybe stretch you until you squeal for me, what do you think?" I said, forcing my two fingers into her ass and spreading my fingers apart as far as I could while my other hand began to rub her clit. She moaned and panted shallowly before trying to reply.

"Yes, Mommy," Summer moaned, making me laugh.

"Yes, Mommy, what baby girl, are you just saying yes Mommy because you've forgotten my question? Does doing this make you remember?" I said, pushing two fingers into her wet pussy and pushing my other two fingers into her ass, making her squeal.

"Yes, Mommy, I'll take it and squeal for you," Summer said as I began to fuck her roughly. I could see the water level rising, and I edged her until the water was halfway filling the tub. Taking my fingers away from her, she moaned in frustration, making me laugh as I picked her up and placed her in the tub.

"Get nice and clean for me, little one," I said before leaving her to wash.

When I came back ten minutes later, she was playing with the bath ducks I had bought her.

"Katy is very happy to have stopped playing hairdressers baby girl," I said, putting her butterfly clips back in the draw. Summer giggled and splashed water over the tub and onto the floor as she raced two ducks around the bath.

"Come on, up you come," I said, placing a towel on my chest and picking her out of the bath. I liked that I was so much bigger than her and that she was unable to fight me. She had tried to resist me a few times, wanting to stay in the water or not wanting to go to bed, but between simply picking her up or placing my thigh over her body to pin her down, she was helpless against me.

"Mommy, I don't have a diaper tonight, I don't need one," Summer said. She looked at me with a wicked brattiness, and I knew that tonight would be fun. I ignored her and took her to my room and threw her down on the bed.

"Did you hear me, Mommy?" Summer said, trying to sound authoritative. I laughed.

"Yes I heard you baby girl, I just don't fucking care what you want. I want you in a diaper, so you'll get a diaper. Maybe I might even put two on you for being such a naughty little girl," I said, taking off my pants. I watched as Summer watched me undress and I enjoyed putting on a show for her. Music or not, I loved how I moved my body until I was standing over Summer's pretty mouth and lowered my cunt onto her lips.

"Lick it for Mommy," I instructed, groping my tits as Summer's tongue dived into my aching hole. I loved smothering her but lifted my thighs, letting her breath before lowering myself onto her again. I kept my hand around her neck, feeling her pulse to make sure she could breathe as I forced her to eat my pussy, rocking back and forth and grinding down on her little face.

"You can't get away from Mommy baby girl, stop trying," I said as I saw her legs start to wriggle. I lifted off her slightly as she gasped for air, my juices covering her face and neck.

"You'd better make me cum little girl," I said, reaching down and slapping her legs apart. I spat on her pussy and rubbed her clit until I felt her moaning into my pussy.

"You're going to cum for Mommy. Say, Mommy, please, baby girl," I commanded, slapping Summer's pussy before finger fucking her again.

"Mommy, please," Summer breathlessly moaned, her lips vibrating against my clit, making my juices flow again.

"Louder," I said, fucking her more roughly, wanting her to be limp with exhaustion.

"Mommy, please!" Summer screamed into my cunt as we both came hard at the same time. I liked feeling my cunt squirt into her mouth and felt her tongue lick me clean as I patted her pussy before wetting a black bunny tailed butt plug with her cream.

"Take it, my pretty girl," I said, pushing it into her resisting ass. I muffled her cries with my pussy as I filled her only recently deflowered asshole with the toy and stayed on top of her until her cries only came as whimpers.

"Good girl," I said slowly. I got off her and picked her up

and cuddled her as I walked into her playroom. I kept cradling her in my arms as I filled her mouth with my nipple and let the weight of my breast fall on her chest and face.

"Suck on, Mommy, baby girl. I know your pretty ass hurts, but you're such a good girl for Mommy," I said. Leaving my nipple in her mouth until she had calmed down, I walked over to the cupboard and picked out her outfit. A pink diaper that I had previously cut a hole in the back to fit her little tail for and a baby blue long sleeve shirt. Tonight I'd leave her braless and took out the nipple clamps. I took out a paci gag and leather cuffs and enjoyed the look in her eyes as she saw just how used she was going to be tonight. Holding my breast in both her hands, she took my nipple out her mouth.

"Mommy, I," Summer started to say before I pushed my nipple back down her throat.

"I don't remember asking your opinion, little one," I said, pinching her nose closed and making her gasp around my breast.

"Much better," I said, holding her in one arm as my other hand slapped her cheek while she suckled. Growing bored of denying her, I put her down on the floor and began diapering her. She wriggled, which just made me shake my head at her and take out a fat vibrating dildo, spitting on it and forcing it up her cunt.

"You're a silly little girl sometimes, baby," I said, turning it on and fastening her diaper in place. I took the nipple clamps and bit down firmly on her nipples, making them hard as I secured the clamps in place.

"Pretty girl," I said as I watched Summer roll around on the floor in sexual frustration. I knew she wouldn't be cumming for at least an hour, and I was going to enjoy every minute of her torture. Next, I put her shirt on and flicked the clamps as I dressed her.

"Please, Mommy please," Summer begged as she tried to touch her pussy through her diaper.

"I knew I'd need these," I laughed, taking her wrists and cuffing them behind her back. I lifted her and took her to the living room. I placed her gently down on the sofa and let Katya out for her nightly prowl. Summer moaned loudly on the couch when I turned the intensity of the vibrator up, and I gagged her, making her suck on the pacifier as her juices dripped into her diaper.

"Who's my slutty baby girl," I said coming to sit behind my pretty toy. I moved her so she was sitting between my thighs and I wrapped my legs around hers, forcing them apart. Summer grunted in defiance, making me laugh and hit her pussy hard over her diaper.

"Give me what I want, baby, you have no choice," I whispered in her ear as I reached around and held her neck while my other hand flicked the clamps up and down. She tried to pull away from me, moaning in tormented frustration before I turned the vibrator onto its highest setting.

"Enjoy my little slut, you can come, you have permission in advance," I said, holding her down and watching the flames of the fire. Summer writhed under me, being forced to cum over and over, the flames from the fire, making the room hot, and Summer began to sweat as she was used. Watching her, I kissed her face and reached into her diaper.

"Mommy is going to finish you off," I said, pulling the vibrator from her pussy before slamming it back into her. She turned in my arms and straddled me, pushing the clamps into my breasts, which just made her squeal behind the gag.

"There it is," I said as I held her on my lap and fucked her with the thick dildo. Pounding into her pussy, Summer fell limp in my arms before she had even cum, and I fucked her defeated body for another hour, filling her hole and feeling her cream squirt out of her used cunt and into her diaper until she shook her head, unable to go on. I smile and gently took the vibrator out of her pussy and undid the gag. She opened her mouth, and I pushed the cock into her mouth, and she held it there like the good little slut she was. I uncuffed her wrists, and she began sucking on the dildo, using both hands like I had trained her too. I smiled and sat against the sofa as I watched her fill her mouth over and over. I let her continue as I took off the clamps, pinching her nipples and pushing the cock down her throat when she flinched.

"I didn't say to stop, did I," I said, ruffling up the fur of her bunny tail. I could tell she could feel the plug moving inside of her by how wide her eyes became when I moved it. I waited until she had sucked all her pussy juice off the toy before I let her stop and picked her up again.

"Time for bed little one," I said, throwing her down and pinning her to the bed with one hand as the other reached into her diaper and pulled the plug out. Summer bit her bottom lip and whimpered as I pulled it from her, making me excited all over again.

"Careful little one, you don't want Mommy to take you again, do you?" I said, coming to cuddle my beautiful baby girl.

Vote One For Mommy

I've never really been into politics. I mean, don't they all promise the same thing and under deliver time after time regardless of who gets elected? Anyway, I always had that view, that was until I met Stacey.

Stacey had been the elected Mayor in a small two-bit town for three years when I rolled in. I'd moved from the city to get some space after a messy breakup and upon arriving, knew this one-horse town would do the trick. It was quiet, the most exciting thing that happened was local boys who drove tractors during the day, chased girls by the lake at night and played football on the weekends. The girls, well, their only real aspiration was to become the wife of whoever the alpha male was of their graduating class, so I knew I'd have no trouble laying low and licking my wounds.

I had been living there for about three months before I ran into her. I was ordering coffee at the one diner in town and saw her out on the street, handing people flyers and pinning on badges.

"Looks kinda lame, doesn't it?" I heard a voice say behind me. I turned around, and there she was. Her beauty had me shook the moment our eyes met. She had that creamy soft type of skin and wave after wave of dark purple hair. Her eyes shone amber as the midday sun shone onto them, and her whole presence was like drinking cool ice tea on a hot day. She must have noticed I was lost for words because she sat down and reached over to take my coffee in her hands. I watched as she took a sip, not minding at all, drinking from a stranger's cup.

"I'm Stacey, who might you be?" Stacey asked, looking at me with a subtle smile.

"Oh, hi, I'm Bianca, but everyone just calls me B," I replied, blushing slightly embarrassed I'd just assumed she'd want to call me B as well. Stacey leaned back, and I was mildly aware that people were staring at us, but I didn't care. Never in my 24 years had I ever had a conversation with anyone as captivating as Stacey.

"Wow, you've lumped me in the everyone box straight off the bat," Stacey teased, only making me more embarrassed. I knew that pleading my case would create a bigger hole I had obviously already dug myself, so I just smiled and looked out the window again. The lady was still there, kissing babies, and it made me wonder what kind of moron would let a Politician kiss their baby.

"Weird, huh?" Stacey asked, interrupting my thoughts. I turned and looked at her blankly after being ripped out of my thoughts. She tilted her head to the woman outside.

"I never kiss babies; in fact, I have a completely different pre-election game plan. Hers is weak," Stacey explained. I looked at her with her mid 30's youth and outlandish hair color and looked back out to the woman on the street.

"You mean, you are running against her?" I asked, unsure of what she was trying to say. My confusion made Stacey laugh, and she nodded.

"I'm the Mayor around here. Didn't you know?" Stacey asked, helping me to finally understand why people were looking at us. They weren't looking at me so much as looking at her.

"Politician, huh," I said, not being quite sure where to place this new information.

"So, your game plan is to drink newcomers coffee and rip shreds off the opposition?" I teased. Stacey laughed, and I caught myself having that awful feeling. The one that latches onto your heart and races through your body, the feeling that only leads to heartbreak.

"No, this is me trying to flirt with you. But clearly, it's not working. Let me try again, would you like to come to dinner on Friday night?" Stacey asked. I couldn't believe the nerve of this woman. I sat back in the booth and looked her up and down. I didn't like how much power she had over me.

"I'm busy, sorry," I said, getting up and leaving the bill on the table with a generous tip. For a family-owned joint, they did a great job.

"What are you so busy with?" Stacey asked. I wasn't

expecting her to keep trying, hell if someone had shut me down the way I was her, I'd of wanted to disappear and never been seen again. I looked at her and tried to study her face. What is it about this one? I thought to myself. A waitress dropped a tray of forks, startling me out of my trance, and I quickly wrote down my number on a napkin.

"Here, give me a call, and we can arrange something," I said, sliding her the napkin with my name and number before I pulled my coat on and walked out the door. I didn't need to turn around to know her eyes were on me; I could feel them. Her stare had been playful and mischievous like she knew I'd give in to her, but there was something else. A daring, a challenge, she looked at me as though she knew my deepest secrets and was waiting for me to discover them too.

A week passed, and I hadn't heard from Stacey. It hurt the first few days, but I just filed it under, typical female bullshit, and got on with the rest of the week. I'd found a job at the local library and enjoyed being to hide all day in the shelves and books. The only other person who worked there was an older lady who had probably only hired me, so she had someone to talk to. I didn't mind, though, and our hour-long conversations over tea and cake made me forget for a moment what I had left behind. She told me about the history of this town, who the true owners of this land were, and who the key players were. Like all small towns, the "founding families" thought they were more important than everyone else and owned most of the commercial real estate.

"What about Stacey?" I asked her during one of our cake and tea breaks. She smiled behind her cup, and it made me wonder what kind of evil this older woman had seen.

"Why do you ask about her?" She replied. I was aware she had answered my question with a question and knew that whatever she told me would have multiple meanings.

"I think you know by that look on your face," I bluntly replied. She put her teacup on the saucer and looked at me, almost as if she was trying to read my mind.

"Be careful with her; she is a powerful woman and will stop at nothing to get what she wants," the woman replied, matching my seriousness. She got up and began putting the books back away, signaling that it was the end of our conversation.

I had all but given up on Stacey when my phone rang one lazy Saturday morning.

"Oh, I haven't interrupted something important, have I?" Stacey asked. I could tell by the fake concern in her voice my response would not shift her desire, so I lied in my reply.

"No, I was just doing some housework," I said then held my breath. She was the sort of person you desperately wanted to be liked by, and I could feel myself getting sucked into her trap.

"Well then, how about after you finish, we go for a walk around the lake. It's beautiful this time of year," Stacey replied before quickly adding, "I'll see you in two hours by the south side dock," before hanging up. I knew she was bad news. I could feel it in my blood, but there I was, two hours later waiting for her. She reminded me of the woman I had spent months hiding from, the one who had taken me in and created a safe space for me to turn that space into a nightmare. I knew the look Stacey had in her eyes, I'd seen it before, but I couldn't seem to shake it. I decided it was best to stay away from her, and I turned around to go back to my car but saw her walking towards me. Damn, I thought to myself.

"Hi there," Stacey said, pulling me into her and kissing me on the cheek.

"Aren't you just the cutest," she said, holding my hand and taking a long look at me. I wasn't wearing anything particularly special, just some baggy jeans and a t-shirt, my hair in a ponytail, and a navy cap. I had decided it was warm enough to wear my new orange flip flops so my toes where freshly pedicured. I guess I did look good, but she looked at me as though she was about to devour me. Our opinions didn't match.

"Thanks," I said as she took my arm in hers and began slowing walking around the lake.

"Who hurt you, baby," Stacey suddenly said, breaking the

silence and making me pull away from her, my guard going up instantly. I looked at Stacey, full of rage.

"What the fuck is your game?" I said, almost growling at her. Stacey's gaze softened from its usual playful challenge, and she slowly reached for my hand.

"I can tell I'm not the first person to call you baby, B," Stacey said tenderly.

"First of all, you don't know shit, and secondly, I'm out," I said, turning and leaving her standing alone.

I was almost back at my car when I heard her running after me. I had half a mind just to ignore her and drive away, but something made me stay. I turned around and saw her doubled over and panting.

"Just...wait," Stacey panted. I waited, but I also watched. I watched how to had to take deep breathes to regain her composure, I watched how she had to pace up and down with her hands on her head to get her breathing under control, but I watched how she changed from her usual arrogant demeanor to something kind and soft.

"Why do I excite you?" I asked just before she was about to speak. Stacey closed her mouth and looked at me, and I could tell she was tossing up, giving me an honest answer or not.

"Honestly, you look like prey, and I'm guessing that's what excites most people. Maybe even the one who hurt you. But I see more than that, and I don't want to hurt the small spaces of you," Stacey said, and I was happy she was honest. I looked down and thought about how to reply.

"So you want to love me, take me home and make me yours?" I said plainly.

"Something like that," Stacey replied, taking a step closer towards me.

"Don't," I said, making her stop.

"Gosh, you're just like a little pound pup, all angry and snappy," Stacey said.

"Yeah, so back off and give me time," I replied, happy to see her nod her head and take a step back. We stayed like that, just looking at each other and resting in each other's energy.

"You wanna tell Mommy what happened, baby?" Stacey said as the sunset. She had come to rest on the side of my car and had stood beside me, watching the sun dip behind the mountain range.

"Not really," I said, resting my head on her shoulder. She reached up and stroked my cheek affectionately and didn't seem to mind me flinching under her touch.

"I'm not going to hurt you, sweetheart," Stacey said, standing up and turning to face me.

"That's what she said too," I replied. Stacey waited for me to speak again, and when I didn't, she reached her hands into her pockets and rocked back and forth on her boot heel.

"Aren't you cold?" Stacey said, shivering. I hadn't noticed

the weather change until then.

"But I don't want to leave," I replied, giving her a chance.

"Then let's not, but could we go somewhere warm?" She asked. I liked that she asked me instead of just planning it. I nodded and unlocked my car, but she waited until I smiled at her, and she got in.

"Where are you taking me, baby?" Stacey asked, reaching for my hair to stroke. I didn't flinch this time. I smiled and moved my head to find her hand.

"Mine," was all I said in reply. I drove in silence, and Stacey seemed to think that was her cue for sharing her expertise with me.

"I've done this a couple of times before. I like having a baby to look after, and I knew you were a little girl the minute I saw you. I couldn't figure you out though, like usually babies don't make me wait to love them. Usually, it's me pushing them away because they get too attached too quickly," Stacey said as I took a long way home. Not because I didn't want her in my space, but because I was enjoying her rambling and found her voice sexy.

"But you, you put me on ice straight outta the gate, and I figured someone like you ending up in a town like this wasn't for any good reason, and when you were flinching before...I'm sorry someone hurt you," Stacey continued. I pulled into my driveway and turned to her, turning the car off.

"It wasn't just someone. It was a list of someone' because I let them. I'm trying to break that pattern. So, don't be like them, because I'm not trying to recreate my past anymore," I stated. Stacey nodded and followed me inside.

"I hope you know nothing is going to happen, Stacey, tonight," I said, leading her through the house, giving her a quick tour.

"I know that. I honestly don't think anything will happen for a long while yet, but that's just fine with me," Stacey said. I couldn't believe how different she was to the absolute hurricane I had first met. Here she was calm, patient, and almost soothing.

"Here," I said, passing her a beer and clinking the top of hers with mine. She smiled and drank deeply before looking at me.

"So, I grew up here, but my family comes from upstate. They moved here when I was three, so this town is all I know. I've gone overseas on holidays, but I always come back, it's got that magical feel to it," Stacey said, giving me the knowledge I didn't ask for. She looked at me, and I took a deep breath knowing it was my turn now.

"I grew up on the east coast, I'm not telling you where, and I moved here to escape a person who used being a 'Domme' as a cover-up for being simply, abusive," I replied taking another sip of my drink. I could tell she wanted more and decided I'd allow her to have her answers I continued.

"She took punishments way too far for me, isolated me from my friends, and said awful things about my family. She didn't listen to my concerns and didn't respect my limits and tried to dominate the things I didn't submit to her. She wasn't like that at the beginning so I stayed with her thinking that she'd go back to who she was when we first got together and it took me way too long to realize that she was never kind or caring or loving, that it was just her way to lure me in," I replied. Stacey had finished her beer by the time I had finished telling her my story, and she listened fully, making me nervous about having someone so present.

"That's worth hiding from," Stacey replied. I like that she didn't try to touch me. I looked at her, and she smiled at me, making my heart flutter.

"And there you were, with all your bravado and confidence, do you see why I ran from you?" I asked, making Stacey laugh.

"Bravado?" She questioned, nodding her head, accepting my judgment.

"Well, bravado aside, I've liked this. We should do it again sometime," Stacey said, getting up and heading to the door, not wanting to outstay her welcome out. She reached for the door handle, and our hands touched as my hand found it's placed on top of hers, making her turn to me.

"Don't," I said this time making her unsure of what I was

meaning. Stacey didn't seem to mind as I took her hand and led her to my room.

"B, I," Stacey started to say but was cut off by my kiss. I liked that she tried to push me back before she got lost in my kiss and reached around to hold me close to her. Her breath was hot on my neck as she held my head and kissed down my body.

"You are beautiful," she whispers, stopping herself as she grabbed the top of my jeans, pulling a fist of denim passionately wanting to be let in but accepting when I shook my head no.

"Feel this," Stacey said, taking my hand and placing my fingers on her pulse.

"I'm racing," she added, making me pull away slowly and look at her.

"You stopped," I said happily, making her confused.

"Of course I did," Stacey replied as if it was the only option in the world.

"You asked me to, remember?" She said, making me laugh.

"Yeah, I'm just happy you did," I said, sitting on my bed.

"I'm not a rapist; only rapists don't stop. You can't call them anything but that if they don't stop when you ask them too little one," Stacey said, laying down next to me. She pulled me close, and I snuggled into her, noticing her sweet perfume for the first time. I buried my face between her warm breasts and let her stroke my hair as she slowly rocked me.

"I know you're going to be guarded for a long while yet, baby girl, but Mommy is here now, and I'll wait for you, always," Stacey said lovingly. I giggled and pulled away to look up at her.

"That should be your campaign slogan, you could be like, vote one for Mommy," I playfully said, resulting in hearing Stacey's hearty laugh and feeling her tickle my tummy.

Baby Girls Get Sippy Cups

"Last drinks," came the routine call from Lacie, the bar owner of the 67th. The 67th was the only bar for miles on a strip of dirt that called itself a road, in the middle of two towns. The 67th had been in Lacie's family for generations, and anyone in 100 miles could tell you about their own story of the 67th.

"To the big fella," someone yelled, and the local crowd raised their glasses to the photo of Lacie's Dad which hung over the beer taps. This always happened after the last drinks were called, and she had grown to love the way her Father was remembered. Closing the bar, Lacie walked out to the carpark and smiled up to the stars. Her father had been gone for five years now, but every night it felt like he was still there, shining in the bright stars over the desert dunes and wiping their faces with sand as he used to with the bar towels. He was always so playful like that, Lacie thought as she sat on her motorbike.

"See you all tomorrow," Lacie said to a group of men still talking out the front as she revved her bike, driving off into the early morning sun as before she could hear their replies.

Lacie tiredly walked into the tattoo parlor a few hours later and fell asleep while her right half sleeve was finished.

"Only Lacie could fall asleep while getting ink done," the artist said, laughing as she worked. She left Lacie in the seat for the next 5 hours, knowing she would be working again that night.

"Whoa, guys, you should have woken me up, sorry," Lacie said sleepily waking up as a customer came in making the bell chime.

"You're right, don't even worry about it," the artist who did Lacie's sleeve replied, receiving a large tip. She looked at Lacie questioningly.

"It's sleep money," Lacie said, laughing before she walked out and got on her bike. She drove to the bar; she knew she didn't have to work for a few hours but didn't mind going in early; it hardly felt like work. It was more how she spent her life. She liked the local guys and their stupid traditions, ongoing pool and darts competitions, and jokes. She liked watching the newly legal kids rock up and try to fit in, nervous about being there or overconfident to try and hide their nerves. She liked watching lovers and fly throws, the people that needed a drink, and people that used it as medicine. She liked it all, and yet, it felt hollow. It didn't matter how those nights were filled, who she gave free drinks too, who she made sure got home safe or who she threw out when the lights got turned off, and the sun came up, it was like she had been in a dream.

Lacie restocked the bar and waited for her 7 pm regulars, setting up their snacks in their spots knowingly. She had turned around to pour herself a shot of tequila and choked on it as she turned back to see a blonde hair girl with brown eyes staring back at her.

"Jesus girl," Lacie coughing and hitting her chest to push the alcohol down. The girl looked down and giggled, making Lacie smirk back once she had stopped coughing.

"I'm going to need some ID sweet thing," Lacie said, shaking her head, disbelief that this girl could be a minute older than 21. The girl rolled her eyes, just adding to Lacie's amusement, and slid her ID over the bar.

"Some face you've got there," Lacie said, quickly calculating the girl's 26 years of age.

"Yeah, I get that a lot," the girl replied. Lacie leaned back against the shelf of spirits and slung the bar towel over her shoulder.

"What'll it be then?" Lacie asked. She saw a couple of regulars make their way in and was happy they knew better than to interrupt her.

"What am I allowed?" The girl replied, making Lacie bite her bottom lip and raise an eyebrow.

"It'll be cocktails all night then, think you can handle that?" Lacie replied. The girl took out a black Amex and flicked it across the bar.

"Can you?" The girl said, making Lacie laugh as she began

making the girl's first drink.

As the night progressed, Lacie made it very clear who her priority was and was happy most people respected that. The locals ordered but didn't make a point of overstaying their welcome at the bar, and Lacie was happy the sweet girl she was happily getting drunk turned down the people who asked her to dance.

"Are you turning them down because you can't dance, or are you worried I'll kick your drunk ass out when you try to stand and fall back down again?" Lacie teased, making the girl take a piece of ice and throw it at her.

"My my baby girl, you are naughty," Lacie said, taking the girl's chin in her hand and making her head shake. Lacie watched as the girl's drunk eyes settled back before she pushed her hair back affectionately.

"I reckon you're done after that one sweetpea," Lacie said, handing the girl, who she had learned was called Cleo, her card back. She never had any intention of charging for this night. Unknowingly, Cleo smiled and put the card back into the top pocket of her denim overalls and happily accepted the water Lacie replaced her unfinished cocktail with.

"This had been fun," Cleo said as she stumbled getting up.

"But I need to go," she added. Lacie nodded knowingly.

"Yeah, I was wondering how long you'd last. The bathroom is just behind that wall there," Lacie said, pointing around to the corner, making Cleo laugh.

"No, I mean, I need to go home," Cleo said, making Lacie wonder how she could hold all those drinks.

"I can't let you drive home, sweetie," Lacie said, snapping her fingers to a guy at the booth who stood up and came to the bar.

"Lock it up for me, I'm taking her home," Lacie said, and the guy, her cousin, nodded and began to get to work.

"You don't have to, I can just catch a taxi," Cleo said, holding onto Lacie as she led her out of the bar.

"Doubt it, there's no taxi's at this hour, baby," Lacie said, going to her bike.

"Here," she said, helping Cleo on. She felt Cleo's body resting on her as she slowly drove off and reached her strong arms around Cleo's body, pulling her close as she turned into the street address Cleo had given her.

"Nice digs," Lacie said, turning the bike off and helping Cleo off.

"Thanks," Cleo sleepily said.

"You can't come in," Cleo said nervously, suddenly very awake.

"Alright, I won't," Lacie said, laughing, wondering why Cleo was so nervous.

"It's not that I don't want you to. It is just that. Um, I, my house is messy," Cleo said, obviously trying to find any reason as not to allow Lacie in.

"What do you think I would do? Just barge in and set up camp?" Lacie said, kissing Cleo on her forehead.

"I'm glad you're home safe, bring your cute self back to mine some time," Lacie said, turning on her heel and heading back to her bike. Cleo stayed standing by the front door as she watched Lacie drive off into the night before she quickly opened her door and felt her diaper become wet under her overalls.

Lacie hadn't seen Cleo for a couple of weeks and had all but given up having a second chance with her when Cleo was suddenly sitting in front of her one quiet night.

"Jesus, will you stop doing that," Lacie said, once again chocking on her drink.

"I am just sitting here, you're the one who is not aware of what's going on around you," Cleo said cheekily.

"Is that so," Lacie replied. Cleo smiled and pointed to the premixed drinks in the fridge.

"No cocktails tonight?" Lacie laughed as she passed Cleo a pink bottle of premixed vodka and raspberry flavoring.

"No, definitely not!" Cleo exclaimed, sipping her drink and looking at Lacie.

"I felt it, you know," Lacie said, taking a gamble. The night she had ridden Cleo home, she had felt the softness of her diaper when she had turned into the corners and held Cleo close.

Knowing she was right in her guess by Cleo's fearful eyes and stunned silence, Lacie smiled.

"You don't have to be worried, I think it's cute," Lacie said making Cleo breath again but look around nervously.

"As if I'd out you little girl," Lacie said, placing her hand on top of Cleo's, happy when she didn't pull away.

"Is that why you didn't want me to come in?" Lacie near whispered. Cleo nodded her head and looked down.

"I kinda don't know what I'm doing with it, I'm sorta new," Cleo whispered back.

"I don't think there's a right or wrong way baby, there's just your way," Lacie said tenderly making Cleo smile and sit back.

"So, what now?" Cleo said, wondering what all this meant.

"Hold that thought," Lacie said as she spent the next 20minutes serving an out of town football team who seemed to make it their nights mission to drink the bar dry.

When Lacie turned back to where Cleo had been sitting, she saw an empty chair. Rushing out from behind the bar, she ran out to see Cleo leaning on her bike.

"Baby," Lacie said involuntarily, relieved Cleo wasn't gone.

"Want to go?" Lacie asked as she walked over to Cleo, who was nodding her head.

"Can I come in this time?" Lacie asked, buckling a helmet

under Cleo's chin.

"Maybe," Cleo replied cheekily, giving Lacie the feeling that a maybe was going to turn very quickly into a yes. Lacie knew she didn't have to drive slow, and this time raced through town, enjoying Cleo's giggles in her ear as she rested her head on her shoulder. Arriving at Cleo's home in no time at all, Lacie took her helmet off and walked her to the door.

"Well goodnight," Lacie said, pulling Cleo into her for a hug. She took her time before she let Cleo go, slowly but very purposely running her fingers through her long blonde hair, grabbing a fist full and pushing her face into her chest as her other hand grabbed her ass and squeezed making Cleo gasp and push her pussy onto Lacie's thigh.

"Don't stop," breathed Cleo as she reached for her keys in her jeans pocket and tried to open the door.

"I was hoping you'd say that," Lacie said as she dipped her head and brought Cleo's mouth up to hers, kissing her passionately as the door opened behind them, making them fall into the house. Lacie kicked the door shut once they were both inside and pushed Cleo onto the floor as she began to ravish her body. Letting her body fall onto Cleo's, Lacie used her knee to nudge Cleo's thighs apart and flexed her quad against Cleo's pussy, making her moan. Lacie kissed down her neck and held Cleo's head gently in her arms as she began to rhythmically pound her thigh against Cleo's pussy, making her gasp each time she was thumped. Cleo reached down to unbutton her jeans, wanting the release to come faster. But Lacie took her hand and held her wrist down, looking into her eyes.

"Alright?" Lacie asked, hoping Cleo was happy to submit this to her. Cleo nodded as she was pounded by Lacie's muscular thigh, grinding down on it and feeling her clit be teased edging her and keeping her there, frustrating her beyond belief.

"Are you going to be Mommy's good girl tonight baby," Lacie whispered in Cleo's ear as she just moaned in response, rolling her head back and closing her eyes.

"Ask Mommy if you want to cum baby," Lacie said as she felt Cleo grab at her full tits as she shuddered and tried to fight her orgasm.

"Please Mommy," Cleo desperately begged breathlessly, a low moan escaping as Lacie whispered, "Yes," in her ear as she moved her arm from around Cleo's head and gently rested her hand on her neck, not sure how much she liked or if this was OK at all. Cleo grabbed her hand and pressed it firmly down on her neck, and Lacie smiled as she took the hint and squeezed tightly, making Cleo's eyes open widely as she came. Swallowing hard and trying to lift her hips under Lacie's body wanting a quicker release Cleo groaned in frustration as she was forced to come slowly. Lacie smiled in satisfaction as she kissed Cleo passionately, enjoying feeling Cleo's breath coming in short, shallow gasps.

"Show Mommy Cleo," Lacie said, unbuttoning Cleo's jeans and letting her finally take them off. Cleo reached down and practically ripped them off her but froze when she realized that Lacie could now see her diaper. Lacie kissed Cleo loving on her cheek as she placed her hand on the front of Cleo's diaper and rubbed her slowly.

"Don't be nervous. You look cute," Lacie said, looking down at Cleo's worried face. She turned her head and looked away. Lacie got off her and sat back as Cleo rested on her elbows.

"I really liked that, but I am kinda exhausted now, Mommy," Cleo said, hesitantly saying, mommy. Lacie hurried over to where she was resting and held her in her arms.

"Then tell me what you need now," Lacie said, making Cleo melt into her arms.

"You mean you don't want to go?" Cleo asked, looking up at Lacie, who shook her head no.

"I want to stay, if you'll let me," Lacie replied. Cleo rolled her body into Lacie's, who held her for a long time. As her ass became numb from sitting on the floor for so long, Cleo stood up and reached for Lacie's hand.

"Shower?" Cleo asked. Lacie followed Cleo to the bathroom.

"I like calling you, Mommy," Cleo nervously said, hoping Lacie liked it too.

"That's nice since that's my name," Lacie said. Cleo

started to take off her clothes but was stopped by Lacie.

"Let me," she said, lifting Cleo's shirt over her head. Cleo giggled as Lacie ran her fingernails over her body, giving her goosebumps. Lacie took off Cleo's diaper and watched as she got into the shower and began to wash.

"You are a beautiful baby girl," Lacie said, almost in a trance looking at Cleo. It made her smile, and she drew a smiley face on the glass shower screen as the room began to get hot and steamy.

"I'm not sure what to do next," Cleo said to Lacie.

"What do you mean?" Lacie replied, taking off her clothes and joining Cleo in the shower.

"Well, do we keep going with the baby stuff, or do you wanna stay the night? Like, what do we do?" Cleo explained. Lacie used Cleo's body wash as she thought about what to do next.

"What space do you feel like you are in?" Lacie asked, making Cleo think for a second.

"A big girl one," Cleo replied, moving so Lacie could rinse off.

"Do you want to stay there? Or do you want to be Mommy's good little girl?" Lacie asked as the water flowed over her athletic body, making her skin glisten.

"Mommy's good girl," Cleo said, shifting her feet nervously, hoping Lacie would be down for it.

"Good," Lacie replied, making Cleo give a sideward smile.

"Let me dry you off before you go to get what you want me to dress you in tonight. Make sure you bring me a diaper, I don't want my little girl going to bed without one," Lacie said, making Cleo's mouth gaped open with just how Mommy like Lacie suddenly sounded.

"Oh baby, does it sound just like you always hoped it would?" Lacie questioned, making Cleo nod her head as Lacie dried her and gently slapped her ass as she left the bathroom to follow the instructions Lacie had given.

Cleo waited patiently in her room for Lacie, who appeared 5minutes later. She was wearing a towel wrapped around her waist, her abs and strong arms made Cleo blush. Lacie didn't say anything as she went to Cleo's cupboard and put on one of her t-shirts and a pair of short pajama shorts.

"Now, what does the baby have for Mommy?" Lacie asked, turning to face Cleo. Cleo held up what she had picked and giggled with Lacie, jumped on her bed.

"Then lay down so I can get you ready little one," Lacie said as Cleo obediently laid on her back.

"What a good girl," Lacie tenderly said as Cleo stayed still while Lacie diapered her. It was the first time Lacie had done anything like this and was impressed with herself how naturally it came. She took the colorful dino onesie and gently dressed Cleo.

"There, Mommy's little princess is almost ready for bed. Have you forgotten something, though, baby?" Lacie asked. Cleo looked around her room and wondered what Lacie could mean.

"Here, open wide little girl," Lacie said, taking a fistful of Cleo's hair and pulling her head back. Cleo gasped, and Lacie took the opportunity to put her pacifier in her mouth before letting her hair go.

"Now you are ready for little bed, girl," Lacie said, snuggling into bed with Cleo. Cleo pushed her face into the side of Lacie's full breast, happily snuggling into it.

"Next time you come into the bar, you'll get your drink in a sippy cup, little miss, baby girls get sippy cups," was the last thing Cleo heard before she fell asleep.

High School Reunion

I had done the usual things after High School, got a part-time job, went to University, graduated, and now worked in the profession I had studied for. I enjoyed holidaying with friends or traveling alone, nothing overly extraordinary but still what I would consider a nice life.

It had been ten years since I had graduated from High School, and I could feel the reunion vibes a month before I got my letter in the mail. High School, gross, I thought to myself as I opened the envelope. I was the loser in High School, the one which even the other bully victims didn't want to hang out with. I had overheard how a popular girl once said she couldn't decide if she'd go to this party or that one and I remember wondering what it must feel like to be invited to so many parties you could choose which one you wanted to attend. I'd never been invited to a party, and I had a sneaky suspicion the only reason I'd been invited to the reunion was an emailing glitch.

As the evening of the reunion approached, I was still unsure if I should go or not. I couldn't help but wonder how everyone had turned out. I wondered if the popular girls were still the beautiful ones or if my career as a makeup artist had given me the lifestyle that surpassed theirs. Ten years ago, I would not have believed anyone if they had told me where I would be today. Back then, I was the orphaned daughter of a crack-addicted mother who didn't know who my Father was, living in foster care with five other kids and wondering where my next meal would come from. I had taken all the pain of being freezing in the winter because my clothes weren't warm enough and falling in love with my gym teacher because she was the only person who had ever shown me kindness and turned my life into something little girls dream about. I had gone to Paris and Milan for fashion week for the last five years, met the most incredible people I could call my friends, and never had to worry about staying warm or having enough food. I still shied away from romance and had only had a handful of romantic encounters, and if I'm honest, those people looked like my high school gym teacher.

She would always wear these mid-thigh black shorts and some colored t-shirt with sneakers that matched. Her hair was always out, and only when she'd get really into a game would she put it up, flexing her big muscular arms as she did so. She'd caught me staring at her several times, but she always just smiled and didn't embarrass me about getting caught. When the other girls had excluded me in a game, she'd change the game so that there were no teams, and although I knew she was just a good teacher, I loved her kindness. She had a deep laugh and a serious, stern voice that even made the boys taken her seriously.

I shook my head, trying to stop thinking about her and put the reunion letter down. I still had four days to think about going or not, and I had to get to work.

Four days came faster than I had thought, and although I'd RSVP'ed I was going, I still was unsure. What if it is just like high school all over again? What if they laugh at me? Wait, laugh at me for what? Driving a Lambo? Holidaying in the Caribbean? They've got nothing on me now, I thought, checking myself. My makeup was, obviously, flawless, and I had bought a black backless dress for the occasion. Teamed with strappy metallic silver heels and a silver clutch, I looked wonderful. However, I couldn't stop the slight tightening of my stomach as nerves raced through my body. Wishing I could take a shot of tequila before I drove, I put the bottle down and made my way to the party.

This was a huge fucking mistake, I said to myself as I walked up the long path that led up to the school. I had to park down the bottom of the hill, and although my heels were comfortable, I felt shaky on them. I passed the tennis courts where I use to play tennis, and the memory of the popular girls deliberately hitting me with the ball came into my mind. Forget that; it's over now. They can't hurt you anymore. I thought as I approached the entrance to a building, which was where I was meant to be going.

There was a woman standing out the front with a table set up and balloons tied to the ends.

"Name?" The woman said in a bubbly voice. Before I could say my name, she was already gasping and holding her hand to her chest.

"Hayley? Hayley Swanston?" She asked. I looked at her and couldn't remember her name to save myself.

"Yes?" I replied, wishing she would tell me her name. Seeing that I had forgotten, she rolled her eyes.

"Sophie McBridge! We use to play tennis together!" The woman replied joyfully. I remember what Sophie McBridge used to look like, and this woman standing in front of me was a far cry from any of my memories. The Sophie that I remember was slender and athletic; this woman was a solid three past Sophie's wide with eyes that were sunken in.

"Oh, Sophie, right sorry, gosh it's been such a long time," I replied, unsure of what to say. Sophie just nodded her head and handed me my name sticker. I looked at it and looked back at her, and she took it from my hands and placed it just above my right breast, rubbing it down.

"There, you're ready to go, top floor, the view is fantastic," Sophie said knowingly, and I just smiled as I walked inside and found the elevator. Holy shit, Sophie McBridge, I thought as the elevator made its great ascent.

Reaching the top, the doors slid open, and a party in full swing greeted me. It was a lot to take in all at once. There was music playing and people mingling, and I just wanted to turn and run away, but as I was about to, I saw on the projected wall display of photos from my tennis days. I walked over to the wall and stared at the girl who stared back at me. With eyes that begged for love, anyone's love, I looked at that girl and wished I could have told her then what I know now.

"Wow, Hayley?" A high pitched voice cut through the masses of conversations and music, making me want to run away. I forced myself to turn and look at the tall, slender blonde behind me. She had always been beautiful, with her angular face and full pink lips; it was no wonder she had been the most popular girl in high school.

"Hi Allison," I heard myself say, annoyed at the slight yearning in my voice for her approval. She looked me up and down and stepped forward, embracing me as though she hadn't spent the better part of our high school years together, making my life a living hell. I held my breath during the embraced but gasped when she pinched my waist with both her hands.

"Not the little chubbsie anymore," she said, grabbing at me, making the women who had begun to form around her laugh.

"Remember what we use to call you, little piggy," Allison said, making the woman laugh even harder. I looked at them, and for the first time, I saw them for who they truly were. Ugly, they were plain, old fashioned ugly with a deprivation to try and make others feel ugly to hide the fact that they were awful human beings. I smiled, reclaiming my power, and looked Allison dead in the eye.

"No I don't remember, I am too busy driving my Lambo and being gifted tickets to events you could never pay for to worry about what some stupid, ugly, never gonna come up bitches as you said ten years ago," I said quickly turning away and walking in the opposite direction trying to get away from them as fast as I could.

I made my way to the long table of drinks, which had been set up by the wall-length window overlooking a sports field. Gosh, cool set up, I thought, seeing how the school had changed. They had somehow managed to get a grass field on the top of one of the other buildings, and I suppose during sporting events, this room would be the one to host the VIPs. I was deep in my thoughts when I heard a familiar voice behind me, "Someone learned how to handle herself." I swallowed hard; I knew who this was. Turning around, my beer in my hand, I locked eyes on her. My beautiful gym teacher and her beautiful face.

"Hi, um Ms," I started to say stop when I saw her shake her head.

"You can call me Veronica now, Hayley," Veronica said, making me blush, apparently to her amusement.

"I see not everything has changed," Veronica said, making

me laugh and wish like mad I could stop going red.

"Are you still teaching?" I asked, trying to steer the conversation away from me. Veronica moved her hand behind my back to grab a drink, making me move forward to get out of her way but only resulting in closing the gap between us, making me blush harder. I was grateful she didn't seem to mind.

"Yeah, apparently gym class is my calling. What about you? Where have you ended up?" Veronica asked, taking a sip from her drink and motioning that I should follow her outside. The air was cooler on the sporting field, and I liked that there weren't so many people out here.

"I'm a makeup artist," I replied once we had found our spot. I liked seeing that I took Veronica by surprise.

"A makeup artist?" She asked, choking on her drink.

"Is that so hard to believe?" I questioned. I didn't want her to think I was lying.

"No, it's just, that's a pretty brutal industry, I would have thought you'd want something a little, gentler after everything," Veronica explained. I leaned against a wall and sighed.

"Apparently, pain is my calling," I said dramatically, making her laugh.

"No, honestly, it's a really good job, and I love it. This place taught me all I needed to know about how to deal with bitches and life taught me the rest," I said honestly. Veronica raised an eyebrow and looked impressed.

"Well, cheers to you then little miss," she said, making my heart skip a beat. She must have sensed it because she bit her bottom lip and looked me up and down.

"Don't," I said quietly, pushing her away.

"You're hardly my student anymore; I haven't seen you for ten years. I can look at all of you now if I want to," Veronica said, making my stomach turn.

"I saw the way you use to. I bet you thought about me when you were all alone at night in your room. I bet you still do," she added, taking a step closer and wrapping an arm around my waist. My legs almost buckled as I felt her muscled arm flex against me as she pulled me closer to her. I don't know if it was the alcohol or if seeing her again just blinded my consciousness, but when her lips met mine, I opened my mouth instinctively. I reached up and wrapped my arms around her neck, standing on my tippy toes and moaned in her mouth, feeling her hand on the back of my head, pushing my mouth deeper into hers. I lost grip of my beer bottle, and it fell to the grass as I let the fire of this kiss ravage through my being. Stopping, I pulled away to see that some people had been watching us, and I turned to leave only to feel Veronica grab my wrist.

"Wrong way, sweetheart, my car is over there," she said in her sexy authoritarian manner. I smiled at her and eagerly took the hand she offered for me to hold as she led me down the hill of the sports field to the staff carpark.

The staff carpark hadn't changed one bit, and I giggled to myself, making Veronica look at me playfully.

"I use to walk this way to first period, the long way, just to see if your car was here because I wanted to know if you were here," I said as we walked through the carpark.

"I know. I use to be able to see you search the number plates until you found mine and smile to yourself when you did from my office. It used to be over there, remember?" Veronica said lovingly.

"How come you never tried to find me after I graduated?" I asked, aware of just how little I sounded.

"Because I'm not perverted and you were still a kid even though you thought you were so big and grown-up graduating high school," Veronica said affectionately.

"Anyway, I've got you now, haven't I?" Veronica said, opening her car door and buckling me in. I looked down at her large hands running over my seat belt, and I hoped that she'd want me for longer than just this night.

"Yeah, you do," I said awestruck as Veronica stood up and went to the driver's side. I wish I could have felt less taken by her, but as she placed her hand on my thigh and lifted my dress slowly, I couldn't help but let her have her fun. When we stopped at a red light, she leaned over and kissed me, making my heart flutter like a schoolgirl, and I was grateful I was sitting because my legs would have given way I'm sure. A car behind us beeped their horn, making Veronica break the kiss and laugh as she began driving again.

"You are such a sweet girl in your grown-up dress and pretty heels, Hayley," Veronica said, slowing the car down, as we began to drive into a leafy neighborhood. I didn't know why she was speaking like this, but I liked it. It made me feel protected and safe with her muscular body and dominating presence, being soft and loving just to me.

She stopped the car and snapped her fingers at me when I tried to get out of the car.

"Let me baby girl," Veronica said, making my pussy tingle. I had never had someone display such affection to me before, and it was blowing my mind. I held my breath as she unbuckled my seat belt and looked me in the eye.

"Little girls need their Mommy to help them, baby," Veronica said. She got up and stood back, giving me enough space to get out of the car, which I did without breaking eye contact.

"Mommy?" I softly whispered. I was worried I sounded pathetic, but Veronica just smiled warmly and opened her arms to me.

"Come here, baby, Mommy is here now," Veronica said, and I almost burst into tears as I fell into her arms only to have them close tightly around me. She must have sensed my state of mind because she looked down and placed her hand on the side of my face, raising my eyes to meet hers.

"I'm going to look after you Hayley, if you'd like that. I'd love to be your Mommy, not just for tonight, but for as long as you want me," Veronica said, kissing the tip of my nose. I looked at her and smiled at absolute submission. There was no way I could think of that would make me ever want to stop Veronica making me feel this way. She reached out her hand, and I placed mine in hers, marveling at how even her hands were strong as she led me inside.

"Make yourself at home sweetie, I just need to get a few things," Veronica said as she disappeared. I wandered into the living room and sat awkwardly on the couch and waited for her to return. Coming back into the room, my eyes must have given me away because Veronica laughed and looked down.

"They aren't that exciting baby girl," she said, talking about her comfortable house clothes. She was wearing a loose-fitting t-shirt and a pair of long, gray, fluffy pajama pants. She came and sat next to me, and I reached out to cuddle her involuntarily.

"Oh, you are just the sweetest little one," Veronica said, moving me onto her lap. I liked that she didn't mind me reaching for her. I never wanted to let her go. We stayed like that, me on her lap, her stroking my arms and thighs until I could feel my eyes growing heavy.

"Come on little girl, Mommy needs to get you clean and

out of your very beautiful but very grown-up clothes," Veronica said. I turned my head and looked at her, hoping that what I was about to say would be the right thing.

"Mommy, thank you," I said, looking down and speaking so quietly it was almost a whisper. I felt Veronica envelop me and kiss me all over my face until I opened my eyes and giggled at her, pushing her away to make her stop.

"You're welcome, my little princess. Mommy knew what you needed then, and I guess fate bought us back together when we could be together, and now little miss, you're Mommy's good girl," Veronica said, standing me up and taking me to the bathroom.

"Strip for Mommy Hayley," Veronica said, reaching into her pants and starting to play with herself. I bit my bottom lip as I slowly pulled my dress off until I was standing in front of her with only my crimson lace thong and heels on. Veronica liked what she saw because she reached out and took my hand, pulling me towards her and putting it down her pants. I could feel how wet she was instantly and gasped when she pulled my body into hers. She kissed me as I played with her pussy, enjoying teasing her and feeling her buck against my hand and grind down on it in frustration. She lifted me and held me on her hip as I began to finger fuck her, giving her what I knew she wanted, and she held me with one arm as the other pulled off her shirt. Taking her large breast in her hand, she brought her nipple to my mouth, and I instinctively took it, sucking and pulling on her nipple as I fucked her. Veronica moved, so she was leaning against the wall as she came, holding me close and breathing deeply as the orgasm made her body shake and shudder. I felt her cum squirt out and cover my fingers and wrist, and dirty her pajama pants.

"Did you like that, Mommy?" I giggled, knowing full well she enjoyed herself. Veronica had shut her eyes but opened one and looked at me.

"Yes, baby girl, you made Mommy very happy," Veronica said, putting me back down. She took off her pants, and my panties and heels and ran us a bath.

"Do you want to bathe with Mommy tonight, baby girl?" Veronica said, making me clap my hands excitably.

"Yes, please Mommy," I said, wiggling my toes happily, making Veronica smirk in satisfaction.

"Then come here and let Mommy help you in," Veronica instructed, holding out a hand to me. I quickly took it, and she held my hand firmly as I stepped into the warm soapy water. Sitting down in the tub, I exhaled, closing my eyes and feeling calm for the first time in a long time.

"I was hoping you'd like this baby," Veronica said, breaking the silence. I turned to see she had come into the bath and was sitting behind me. Pulling me into her, she held me by my neck and snaked her hand down my body to my clit, resting there before she cupped my pussy.

"Now Mommy is going to make you pay for teasing me earlier princess, do you think I didn't know what you were doing my little minx?" Veronica whispered in my ear. I leaned back and felt her tits press into my should blades and neck as she began to part my pussy lips and entered me forcefully, making me gasp and moan.

"I didn't say I'd be gentle, did I baby girl. Mommy is going to force so many orgasms on you, and there's nothing you can do about it. I'm going to love you through all of them, but Mommy isn't going to stop until you are limp in my arms, precious baby," Veronica said as she held me in place and began pounding my pussy.

In what felt like no time at all, I was squirming from left to right in the tub, splashing water onto the bathroom floor as Veronica forced the first orgasm on me.

"Shhh, little one, don't try and fight me, Mommy always wins," Veronica said as I panted and gasped at the intensity of my climax. I had never orgasmed so hard before, and I was exhausted after the first one, but Veronica wasn't joking when she said she wouldn't stop and didn't wait more than five seconds until she was fucking me under the water again.

"Mommy, I can't," I breathlessly tried to say as another orgasm took hold of me. I tighten my pussy, trying to stop it from hitting so soon, but Veronica just moved her fingers onto my clit and began rubbing me, making me double over and grab her thighs as it ravaged my body. I loosened my grip and fell back into her as my body quivered and shook in the aftermath of her touch. I looked up at her with pleading eyes only to be met by her kisses.

"Give Mommy one more baby, I know you can give me one more," Veronica said, making me nod my head. I wanted to give her whatever she wanted. I spread my legs and felt Veronica pat my pussy like she owned in and began rubbing me again. I wanted her nipple in my mouth again and pushed her hand away quickly and turned in her arms before she could get mad that I denied her. I straddled her waist and kissed her deeply, feeling her smile and bringing her hand back to force her fingers into me once again. I gasped and bent forward, feeling safe when Veronica placed her hand on my back.

"Come on, baby girl, give it to Mommy," Veronica said, patting my back and pressing her chest toward my mouth.

"Open your pretty mouth for Mommy," she instructed, rubbing her nipple across my lips. I began to suckle just as she began to slide her fingers in and out of my sensitive pussy. She must have felt how tender I was, and this time let the orgasm build slowly, rubbing and stroking my clit tenderly, gently pushing and keeping her fingers inside of me as I began to moan.

"Please, Mommy," I moaned, making her quicken her pace. I wasn't sure how much longer I could take her slow onslaught, but she held me close as my body fell limp on her lap.

All too soon, I began to cry, and Veronica held me tenderly, wiping my tears away and telling me what a good girl I was until I was only snuggling into her neck.

"I have just never felt that before," I said, dropping my hand to play in the water.

"What sweetie?" Veronica asked.

"Kindness," I replied honestly, shifting on her lap to look at her. She smiled and kissed my forehead.

"I know. Will you let me love you a little longer?" Veronica asked. I sat back and ran my hands over her muscley shoulders and arms. I stopped at her abs and looked at her, smiling bashfully when she nodded her head for me to continue. I grabbed her full heavy breasts and traced over the ripples of her abs, stopping at her strong quads.

"I'll let you love me forever, Mommy," I replied, making her smile and splashing me playfully with the now cold water.

Mommy Will Take Care Of It

Savannah had lived by the beach for three years before she met Amber. Her life had been nothing special, but she had a house by the beach, and that suited her fine. She had a job at a local surf shop doing retail and had settled into a predictable, easy kind of life. The only thing Savannah had learned pretty quickly was that her new home didn't have the huge kink scene that had been available to her in the city. Out here, the kinkiest thing a girl had let her do was to tie her down, and even that Savannah didn't find particularly thrilling. What she liked was being a Mommy to a sweet baby girl. She liked to take them in and enjoy them for as long as they would let her. She'd give them baths and make them wear diapers, dress them in cute baby clothes and nurse them until their tummies were full. She would shower them in love and affection until, for one reason or another, they'd leave.

"I just don't get it," Savannah said, talking to her friend Josh on the phone.

"I don't get how I can't keep a baby. They always want you when they are sad, but the minute life seems too easy for them, they are up and outa there. I hate it," Savannah explained. She had known Josh for years, meeting when they were both single, but Josh had long since had a baby girl.

"I don't know; maybe you should be a bit more picky with who you spend your time with. I really wouldn't be so nice to them until they really show you that they want to be with you," Josh said. Savannah took his words to heart and vowed to make it difficult for the next girl to win her over.

"Hi, how may I help you?" Savannah said the next day to a girl how had brought in a broken board. Savannah hated the look of this girl the minute she saw her. She was just the type of girl who routinely broke Savannah's heart. With her tanned skin and sun-kissed face dotted with freckles, Savannah knew why her pulse began to race.

"I got the board home and realized that there was a chip in it, I was just wondering if I could exchange it for a new one?" The girl said. She had a surfers body, toned and lean with sun-bleached blonde hair, wavy from the sea salt. Savannah looked at the board and noticed that it was indeed chipped and hadn't been in the water yet.

"Yeah sure, that's no problem, sorry about that. Let me see if there's one out the back. Feel free to browse while I check," Savannah said. The girl smiled at her, and Savannah wished she could take her out the back and fuck her until she couldn't walk, but she just flicked through the boards until she found the right one.

Taking it back out onto the floor, the girl appeared from behind a shelf.

"Oh, thanks, that's great," she said, looking delighted. Savannah took her to the register and showed the girl how to fill out the paperwork for the exchange and was almost relieved when the girl left. However, that quickly turned into knowing dread when Savannah saw the message the girl had left her, 'Hey Savannah; I'm Amber - you already have my number X,' Shit thought Savannah, nervous that this would lead to another heartbreak.

Savannah decided she would take Josh's advice and not jump into Amber's world headfirst. Instead, she had done the complete opposite and not messaged Amber at all, trying to push her from her mind. A week after Amber had been in the store, Savannah looked up to see her walking in this time with a beach towel she had bought previously.

"Hi, Amber," Savannah said making Amber smile.

"I didn't think you would remember me at all," Amber said, raising an eyebrow. Savannah smirked. She sounds angry, she thought, taking in Amber's attitude.

"Sorry, I've just been really busy. What can I help you with this time?" Savannah said, seeing her boss leave the lunchroom. Amber relaxed and placed the towel on the counter.

"I got this as a present, but I think I'd like to exchange it for another color," Amber said. Savannah nodded and waited for

Amber to turn and look for what she wanted, but she stayed at the counter and just looked blankly back at Savannah.

"Well, are you coming? I need your advice," Amber said, blinking sweetly at Savannah. A familiar stirring began between Savannah's thighs, and she smiled and came out from behind the counter.

"The towels are over here," Savannah said, taking Amber's hand as she passed her and led her to the towels. Amber giggled and smiled up at Savannah, who just rolled her eyes.

"Little girls like you honestly," Savannah said, crossing her arms over her chest and watched Amber take 20 minutes to select a color she liked when she was finally ready to make the exchange Amber grabbed Savannah's forearm and stopped walking.

"What is it, baby girl?" Savannah said involuntarily and held her breath, hoping that Amber didn't mind.

"I was just wondering if there was a new one out the back?" Amber said, relieving Savannah's fears. Exhaling, Savannah relaxed and nodded, turning toward the back room.

"Come with me," Savannah said and took Amber's hand once again. Amber giggled as Savannah pulled her into her the back room quickly, happy that it was a slow day and that no one else was in the store.

"This is naughty," Amber giggled. Savannah reached up and took down a new towel that still had its packaging on.

"Very naughty, do you know what I do with naughty girls, Amber?" Savannah said, a winning smile widening on her face. Amber just shook her head no and held her towel to her chest. Savannah grabbed Amber's shoulder and spun her around, making her face the shelving of the storeroom. Savannah lifted Amber's skirt and was greeted with light pink satin panties that made her moan.

"What a cute little girl you are," Savannah said, trying to decide whether she was going to spank Amber and fuck her but as Amber wiggled her ass for Savannah, her hand came firmly down on Amber's ass making her drop her towel.

"Count them for me, little one," Savannah said as she spanked Amber's panty covered ass.

"1, 2, 3, 4, 5, 6, ouch," Amber said breathlessly. Savannah stopped and rubbed Amber's reddening ass and grabbed her panties, pulling them up and into her ass, making her cheeks bounce.

"That looks lovely my little slut, is that what you do, tease people until they play with you?" Savannah said, aware that she needed to get back onto the main floor soon. Amber bit her bottom lip and just nodded, attempting to turn around and look at Savannah. Savannah placed her hand on Amber's head and turned her face away.

"Did I could say you could fucking look at me, baby girl? I don't let naughty girls look at Mommy," Savannah said, deciding she didn't care how Amber felt about the kink she was forcing on her. Amber just moaned and reached back to spread her ass for Savannah, making Savannah smile and wished she had more time to play with her. Giving Amber's ass one more spank, she took Amber's hands down and pulled her in for a cuddle.

"Come on baby, Mommy has to get back to work," Savannah whispered, kissing her forehead before she grabbed the towel Amber had dropped and took her back out to the main floor. Turned on by the fact that she knew Amber's panties were still up her ass, Savannah wrote her number up Amber's arm and looked into her eyes as she spoke her parting words.

"If you don't call me within the hour, don't bother coming back," Savannah said in a low, commanding voice, making sure no one else heard. Amber just nodded, her wide eyes submitting to Savannah, who just smiled and tilted her head to the door, and Amber followed her instruction to leave.

Savannah finished her shift and checked her phone, hoping that Amber had followed her instruction and called her. Looking down, Savannah was delighted to see that not only had Amber called and left a cute voice message, but had taken a series of photos and sent them as well. Ok, she likes me, thought Savannah as she happily flicked through the slutty photos Amber had sent her.

"Savannah? It's me, Amber," Amber said over the phone

two weeks later. Savannah and Amber had seen each other a couple of times over the last two weeks, and they had agreed to meet up tonight for a movie at a newly built cinema.

"Hi baby girl, are you OK?" Savannah replied, aware that they were met to meet up in a few hours. Amber sniffed, and Savannah could tell that she had been crying.

"I don't think I'll be able to make it tonight, I'm getting kinda sick, and I don't want you to get sick like me," Amber said, getting teary again. Before Savannah could reply, Amber spoke again.

"Sorry I get emotional when I'm sick," Amber said, melting Savannah's heart.

"It's OK baby girl can Mommy come over and make it all better?" Savannah asked, hoping Amber would agree. She could tell Amber was smiling through the phone by her voice when she replied.

"Yes, please, Mommy, I thought you wouldn't want to because you might get sick," Amber said.

"Mommy has to make sure her baby girl is all better, I think I'll be fine, text me your address little girl," Savannah said, feeling her phone buzz with Amber's text.

"Alright, baby, hold on, Mommy is on her way," Savannah said, hanging up the phone and getting ready for a different kind of night.

Savannah arrived at Amber's house within the hour and was happy when she realized that Amber lived in a nice part of their beach town. She had ocean views and a little whitewashed wooden cottage on the top of a hill surrounded by a white picket fence and a gravel driveway. Cute, Savannah thought to herself as she got out and made her way to the front door. Before she could knock on the door, Amber opened it with a smile and a mug of tea. She sniffed and looked apologetically at Savannah.

"I'm sorry, Mommy," Amber said as Savannah walked in and took the mug of tea from Amber's hands.

"It's OK; I guess Mommy has to look after you in more ways than just making sure you buy cute things," Savannah said, realizing the tea was cold.

"Come on, sweetie, let's get this sorted first," Savannah said, gesturing to the tea.

Savannah made Amber a new pot of tea and ran her a warm bath while they waited for the tea to slowly cool to drinking temperature. Undressing Amber, Savannah flicked her nipples until she squealed and pulled away.

"No," Savannah said, waiting for Amber to move back to her previous position. Seeing that Amber wasn't sure what Savannah wanted, Savannah took her wrist and gently moved her onto the floor on her knees.

"Wider," Savannah said, slapping Amber's thighs until she was satisfied.

"You're not so sick that you can't be in position for me, baby girl, and this is how you'll wait for me when I say kneel, do you understand?" Savannah asked Amber, who just nodded. Savannah clawed at Amber's tits until she whimpered.

"Say yes, Mommy if you understand baby girl," Savannah said patiently and looked at the red marks she had made on Amber's soft flesh.

"Yes, Mommy," Amber replied, and Savannah moved Amber's hands onto the back of her head.

"Like this. Make sure Mommy doesn't have to repeat this lesson darling," Savannah said, cupping Amber's chin and gently slapping her cheeks, only stopping when her eyes began to water.

"Darling, you can let me know your limits," Savannah said, hoping that Amber wasn't trying to be too brave.

"Ok, Mommy, but it's OK, I'm just sensitive," Amber said, looking up at Savannah who stood over her. Savannah pulled on Amber's nipples once again and enjoyed seeing them go hard, and Amber bite her bottom lip, trying not to break her position.

"Get in the bath, little one," Savannah suddenly said, remembering that she was meant to be looking after Amber. Amber stood, and Savannah helped her into the bath, poured her a tea, and passed that to her next before beginning to pour warm water down Amber's back, making low moans escape her throat.

"Do you like that baby girl?" Savannah asked, and Amber

began to nod before her eyes popped open as she remembered what Savannah wanted from her.

"Yes, Mommy," Amber quickly said as Savannah bent down and kissed her forehead.

"Quick learner, baby, you're going to make Mommy very happy," Savannah said as she began to rub between Amber's thighs.

"Don't get too excited; I'm not about to fuck you, little horny girl," Savannah laughed, pulling the plug on Amber's bath before she was ready to get.

"But Mommy, don't you want to play with me?" Amber said, letting Savannah dry her off. Savannah was drying Amber's feet and looked up at her with a menacing look.

"Careful what you ask for baby girl. You have no idea how badly I want to play with you, but I'm not about to push you, not when you are sick," Savannah replied. Amber pouted before she had an idea.

"But Mommy," Amber said, taking the towel from Savannah's hands and throwing it on the floor, turning around to face away from Savannah and spreading her ass cheeks showing Savannah her pussy and ass.

"Baby girl, don't tease Mommy," Savannah said, her last warning. Amber giggled and put two fingers in her mouth, sucking and licking them as Savannah crossed her arms and raised her eyebrow.

"Keep going, little slut, and Mommy will finish you," Savannah said, watching Amber squat in front of her and slid her wet fingers into her pussy. Savannah grabbed Amber by her hair and lifted her to her feet.

"You asked for this little slut, Mommy is going to play with you the way I want to, you'd better not resist me," Savannah said dragging Amber to the living room and throwing her down on the couch. Amber turned around, giggling but stopped as Savannah pulled her pants down, and Amber's mouth was covered by Savannah's pussy.

"Worship me, you little bitch, show Mommy why I should spend my time with you," Savannah moaned as Amber licked and sucked on Savannah's pussy. Savannah reached down and pushed two fingers into Amber's tight pussy and enjoyed hearing Amber gasp and groan as Savannah forced her fingers into her.

"Not so wet anymore are you baby girl, Mommy is going to fuck you raw until you are squirting for me," Savannah said and began pumping her fingers roughly in Amber, feeling Amber's panting breath on her pussy as her groans turned into moans and felt her hips buck trying to have Savannah deeper in her.

"Did I say stop bitch?" Savannah growled, taking her fingers out of Amber and slapping her hand on her chest until Amber went back to eating Savannah out with an intensity she was satisfied with.

"Good, pretty little cunt, make Mommy happy," Savannah said as she felt her orgasm hit her covering Amber's mouth in her juices and clenched her thighs together, making Amber swallow her cum.

"Drink me, bitch, what did Mommy say about resisting me?" Savannah said, smiling as she felt Amber nervously begin to swallow her pussy juices.

Getting off Amber's face, Savannah smiled as she saw Amber's wide-eyed submission and cum-drenched chin and tits. Savannah rubbed her hands roughly over Amber's tits and slapped them roughly as she pulled Amber close and held her as she forced an orgasm on her.

"Mommy," Amber whimpered softly as she gripped Savannah's forearms and let her orgasm take her.

"Oh, you are just a sweetheart, aren't you, baby girl," Savannah said, happily seeing how wrecked Amber was after one orgasm.

"We can work on your stamina once you are better, baby girl. Come on, let Mommy clean you again and get you into bed little one," Savannah said she took Amber back into the bathroom.

Mommy Is My Best Friend

"Candi," Mary called as she turned the key to her friend's apartment. Mary and Candice had been friends since they were in first grade. They had been in each other's classes all through school, and when Mary went to Harvard for college, Candice made sure she was eligible for admittance as well. They had shared a dorm room until they both graduated with business degrees and had even started working for the same company. However, what Candice had never shared with Mary, not even once, was that she was a baby. A crayon coloring, diaper-wearing, stuffie cuddling baby. She had loved the times Mary use to come home drunk from a frat party and cuddle in her bed with her or the way Mary would play with her hair, unknowingly putting her in her little space. But between College finishing and Mary's new boyfriend Cam, Candice knew that her cuddling days were numbered.

"I'm in here," Candice called back from the balcony. Tonight they were going to go out for one last girls night before Mary moved to the other side of the city with Cam. Candice hated Cam, not for any other reason except that he was the one person who had been able to take Mary away from her.

Mary appeared at the balcony, and Candice had to catch her

breath by what she saw. Mary had a leopard print wrap-around dress that had a deep V neckline and a hem that stopped just under her ass. Her black high heels made the muscles in her strong thighs push out, and I tightened my pussy, trying to stay calm as she twirled in front of me.

"What do you think?" Mary asked, bending down to kiss me on my cheek. I wish I hadn't blushed; I wished, even more, she hadn't of seen it.

"Oh, you think I'm pretty, I knew you would, I might have dressed for you tonight," Mary teased taking my hand and placing it on her thigh. Pulling away, I looked at her like she had lost her mind.

"Mary, what the fuck?" I asked almost angry that she was so seductive tonight.

"Oh, come on, you can't tell me that after all this time you haven't at least thought about it?" Mary replied, grabbing my drink and finishing it. I shook my head and stood up, wanting to get away from her. Of course, I had thought about it. I'd thought about her in almost every possible position every night since we had been 14, but this was just too much. I couldn't even bring myself to look at her as she came in after me.

"Hey, sorry, I just thought it might be fun," Mary said softly. I looked up at her with tear-filled eyes, and she pulled me in close to her.

"Candi, I'm sorry," Mary said, stroking my hair. I held her, smelling her sweet perfume and letting her nurture me for the longest time before I broke the embrace.

"I've always thought about you, Mary. So doing this would be too much knowing that you were moving away and that it wouldn't mean anything to you," I replied, not daring to meet her eyes, but I could tell she was frowning by the tone in her voice.

"It wouldn't mean nothing to me, you must know that I know," Mary said, making me freeze. I looked at her, and a shiver of terror shot down my body.

"What do you mean?" I replied, hoping she wasn't about to say what I knew she was about to say.

"The blankie, all your excuses for coloring, the fact that you use to suck your thumb when we cuddled together Candi, I know," Mary explained, making me burn red. I pushed her away and ran into my room, shutting the door behind me so Mary couldn't follow.

"Come on, don't be so silly," Mary yelled through the door. It was just all way too much. I couldn't believe she had known all this time. Oh, how I had thought about her being my Mommy and here she was, willing, even teasing me to let her and I just couldn't. I stepped away from the door, and Mary turned the handle, opening the door slightly.

"Will you let me come in?" She asked. I made a noise in my throat; she knew to be yes, and she walked in and shut the door behind her.

"Come and sit with me on your bed, baby," Mary said, making me open my mouth in protest.

"You don't have to do this, Mary," I whispered, embarrassed. She smiled and opened her arms, and I nervously walked over to her.

"You won't need these tonight," Mary said, leaning down and taking off my heels. I let her, still rigid in her arms, unable to relax. Feeling this, Mary began to open her dress.

"I know what the baby needs," Mary said, pushing her breast into my mouth. I tried to resist her, but she held me firmly, and Mary had always been stronger than I was.

"Just suck baby girl, Mommy has been working on a special treat for you," Mary said, forcing me to begin to regress. I could feel it coming, the little space she was pushing me into. As I was forced to suckle on her, I felt it, warm milk. My eyes grew wide, and Mary smiled a toothy grin as I swallowed.

"There you go, baby, drink up Mommy's milk," Mary said, and just like that she had me. I stopped trying to push her away and relaxed into her arms, defeated but feeling very loved. Mary held me close as she began to rock me and loosened her grip, content that I wouldn't try to fight her anymore.

"Good girl. Mommy's clever baby," Mary said, patting my tummy. She held me for a few minutes longer before standing me up and taking off my black cocktail dress and bra. Stopping at my panties, Mary smiled.

"I have something I just know you're going to love, baby girl," Mary said, getting up and walking over to her bag. I hadn't seen it when she had come in, but she had brought over a big baby bag which I could see had a diaper poking out the top. Clapping my hands happily, Mary laughed, coming back and bopping me on the head with a duck stuffie.

"Lie down for Mommy, let me dress you in something more appropriate, baby girl," Mary said, placing a changing mat on the floor. She guided me onto my back, and I reached for the stuffie, excited to play with it.

"There you are baby girl; I told you Mommy had treats for you," Mary said, sprinkling cold powder over me before sticking the diaper tabs down. Next, she took out a white cotton, long sleeve onesie and gently dressed me, clipping the onesies clips securely. Mary left me to play with the duck as she stood up and kicked her heels off. I liked seeing her settle in, knowing she wouldn't leave me.

"What shall we do tonight baby girl, I don't think going out is on the table anymore," Mary asked, sitting down on the couch. I looked up at her and thought about her question. I shrugged my shoulders and went back to playing, making her laugh.

"Well, if you have no ideas, then I guess you're at Mommy's mercy baby girl," Mary said, spanking my ass, making me giggle and try to crawl away from her. She grabbed my ankle and pulled me back to her. Mary held me in one arm as she began to rub herself under her dress.

"You didn't think Mommy would let you get away that easily, did you, princess?" Mary asked, taking my hand and sliding my fingers past her panties. I gasped, surprised how wet Mary was, and she rolled her head back as I began to play with her.

"Don't you dare stop baby girl, make Mommy happy," Mary said, slapping my face when I tried to pull my hand away. I pouted and looked at her, but Mary just grabbed my hand and forced me to rub her harder. She reached over to her bag and pulled out a paddle, and I pushed my fingers into her, not wanting her to use the paddle on me.

"Oh, is someone scared, baby girl?" Mary said, bringing the paddle down on my diapered bottom hard enough for me to jump. I nodded my head and began sucking my thumb as my other hand finger fucked her.

"There is it little one, keep going," Mary said, grabbing me and pulling me onto her lap as she was fucked. Using the paddle on my thighs and ass, Mary began rocking against my hand, and I felt her juices drip down my wrist as she came. Without warning, Mary got up, and I fell on the floor with a thud.

"Get over here," Mary practically barked as she patted her lap. I stood up to feel her paddle on my tummy.

"I said get over here; I never said to stand," Mary said as I dropped to my knees, and she nodded encouragingly as I crawled to her.

"Better," Mary said, grabbing my throat and pulling me onto her lap. I had always loved snuggling into Mary's thighs when we were at the beach or the park having a picnic, but she began touching me in a way she never had before.

"I wonder how much you can take little one," Mary said, spanking me with all her strength, the paddle making a sound so loud I covered my ears.

"Cute little girl, take your hands away for Mommy," Mary said and waited while I nervously took my hands away. Mary paddled me until I was whimpering after each hit; the strength of her arm had me feeling the pain through my diaper. She held my head in her arm, bringing her breast to my mouth and let me suckle as she paddled me over and over.

"Mommy, I can't," I whispered, worried that I was dangerously close to my limit. Mary smiled and squeezed milk into my mouth as she quickly paddled me hard and fast until I squealed and pulled away from her gasping.

"Good girl," Mary said slowly as she looked at me and put the paddle down. My ass was sore and felt red hot as Mary pulled me up and cuddled me again.

"I'm so impressed with you baby; you took so much more than I thought you could. My arm is even sore from the paddling you just took like such a good girl. Did Mommy hurt your little bottom?" Mary asked and took my thumb out of my mouth and replaced it with a purple paci. I nodded, and she kissed my cheeks and forehead as she gently pushed me onto the floor and back onto the changing mat.

"Let Mommy see," Mary said, slowly taking off my onesie and diaper. I could feel the burn of her paddle still on my ass and turned, trying to see how red she had made me, resulting in her slapping my bare ass.

"Mommy," I said, gasped in pain. Mary just slapped me a few more times, holding me in place as she had her way with me.

"It's not up to you, sweetie," Mary said kindly as she kept slapping my sensitive skin, making me whimper and moan.

"Shh, be a good girl for Mommy and take this," Mary said lovingly as she parted my ass cheeks and began rubbing my pussy.

"I knew you loved this Mommy's pretty little slut," Mary said, slapping my ass harder in time to her rubbing my pussy. I didn't think I could last any longer and screamed as I came. I was mildly aware that Mary may have wanted me to ask permission, but I couldn't think that thought through enough to get those words out. So I just lay there, spent and exhausted with Mary slapping my ass.

"You naughty girl, I didn't think I would have to spell everything out to you if you want to cum you ask Mommy for permission first little lady," Mary said.

That was the last thing I remember hearing, but when I heard Mary's voice again, it wasn't the harsh tone she had used with me before.

"Baby girl, Mommy, was so worried," Mary said. She had moved down to lay next to me, and I blinked my eyes sleepily at her.

"If that was too much, you should have said something darling," Mary said before she quickly corrected herself.

"I'm sorry Mommy didn't realize you needed to stop baby, did you push through so I would think you were a good girl?" Mary asked and cuddled me closed when I nodded yes.

"Silly girl, Mommy will always think you are a good girl. I'm proud of you, baby; I won't take it that far again, OK?" Mary said, holding me gently in her arms. She let me bite her breasts before I tried to pull away from her.

"Where do you think you're going, Mommy has to take care of that little ass first baby," Mary said taking out the lotion and laying me on my tummy as she rubbed the cool balm over my hot skin. It felt nice to have her take care of me, and she kissed up my back when she was done.

"Let's get you dressed again, darling," Mary said, going to her bag and taking out a new diaper. She was gentle and soft as she lifted my body with ease and dressed me again before she picked me up and carried me into my bedroom. Placing me on the bed, she pulled back the sheets and cuddled with me.

"I don't want to lose you," I said, burying my head into her ample chest.

"Baby girl, Cam is not the enemy. He already has a baby girl and boy, that's how I met him, I was looking for someone who understood all the things I wanted to do with you," Mary explained making my head swirl.

"I use to watch you while you slept. Stroked your hair out off your face and wrapped you in your blankie. I wanted you then, but I'm claiming you now. Are you going to try and fight, Mommy?" Mary asked. I curled my toes and pouted.

"But I don't want to share you, Mommy," I said, saying Mommy for the first time. It made Mary beam that I had done so, and she wrapped her arms around me, making me feel safe and loved.

"I know you don't baby girl. How about this, from now on, you are Mommy's baby, and we see each other once a week for playtimes. I'll stay over from Saturday Morning to Sunday lunchtime, what do you think?" Mary said. I nodded and clapped my hands happily. This had been my dream, to have Mary as my Mommy, and now it had finally come true.

Who is Tina Moore?

Tina Moore has enjoyed the lifestyle of a Mommy Domme for several years. She began exploring kink and BDSM in her youth and found her love of being a strict Mommy Domme in early 2000. Tina Moore is now an author of many MDLG and ABDL themed novels.

Having enjoyed many years in the kink community, Tina Moore combines these experiences with the sweet and naughty things her baby girl does to bring you tantalizing and salacious stories.

Follow her on:

Author Page on Amazon

Instagram @tinamoore.kdp

www.ingramcontent.com/pod-product-compliance
Lightning Source LLC
Chambersburg PA
CBHW031033190726
48286CB00003BA/1152